A kelpie
shape
It lives in lochs and rivers.

The Linton Worm is a dragon which lives in a hill. It comes out to find animals to eat.

Mermaids are half fish and half human.
They live in the sea.

The unicorn is Scotland's national animal.
They are magical horses which
have a horn on their heads.

Fairies are tiny spirits who
love to dance and do magic!

The Blue Men of the Minch take on the form of water so they can sink ships.

Selkies are also known as
'the seal folk'.
They can change from seals
into people whenever they want.

The Clootie is the
Scottish name for the Devil.

The Ghillie Dhu is an elf
who lives in the woods.
He only comes out at night.

The Old Man of Storr is a giant who lives on the Isle of Skye.

Legend has it that the Cailleach made the hills, mountains and rivers of Scotland.

The Stoor Worm is a giant sea snake which frightens passing ships.

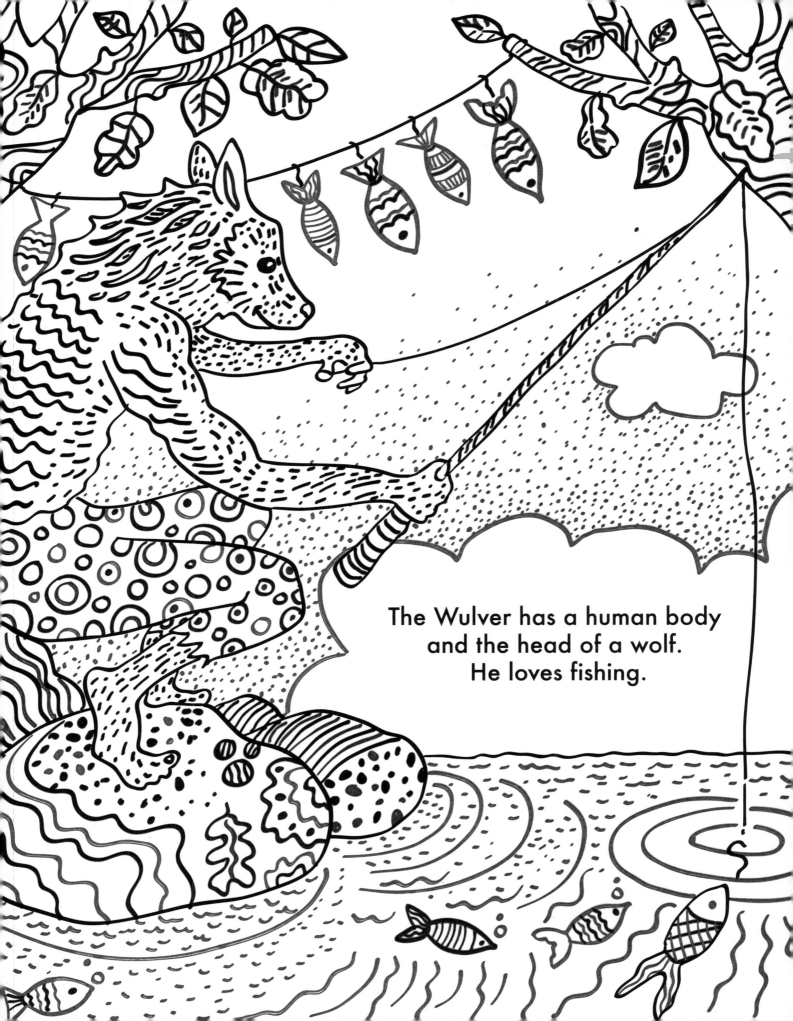

The Wulver has a human body
and the head of a wolf.
He loves fishing.

No one knows whether the haggis really exists or not. If it does, maybe it looks like this.

The Loch Ness Monster
is a mysterious creature which many
people think lives in the
deep waters of Loch Ness.

A broonie is a little goblin
who loves to help with housework!